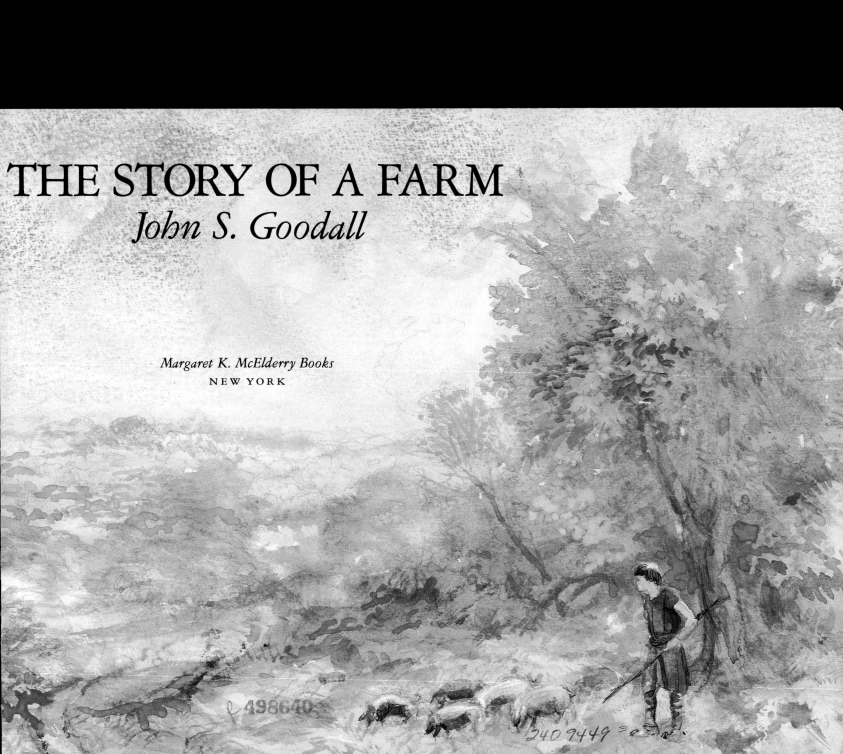

THE STORY OF A FARM
John S. Goodall

Margaret K. McElderry Books
NEW YORK

Margaret K. McElderry Books
Macmillan Publishing Company
866 Third Avenue
New York, NY 10022

First United States Edition
Printed in Hong Kong

10 9 8 7 6 5 4 3 2 1

Library of Congress Cataloging-in-Publication Data
Goodall, John S.
The story of a farm.
Summary: By following the changes in one house over
centuries, the development of farm life in England is depicted.
1. Farm life—England—History—Pictorial works—
Juvenile literature.   2. Farms—England—History—
Pictorial works—Juvenile literature.   3. England—
Social life and customs—Pictorial works—Juvenile
literature.   [1. Farm life—Pictorial works.   2. England—
Social life and customs—Pictorial works]   I. Title.
S522G7G65   1989   630'.942   88–3398
ISBN 0-689-50479-9